Ten in the Bed

Executive Producers: **Kim Mitzo Thompson, Karen Mitzo Hilderbrand**
Music Arranged By: **Hal Wright**
Music Vocals: **The Nashville Kids Sound**
Illustrated By: **Dorothy Stott**
Book Design: **Jennifer Birchler**

Published By:
Twin Sisters Productions
4710 Hudson Drive
Stow, OH 44224 USA
www.twinsisters.com   1-800-248-8946

ISBN-13: 978-159922-503-6

There were **ten** in the bed
and the little one said, "Roll over! Roll over!"
So they all rolled over and one fell out.

There were **nine** in the bed
and the little one said, "Roll over! Roll over!"
So they all rolled over and one fell out.

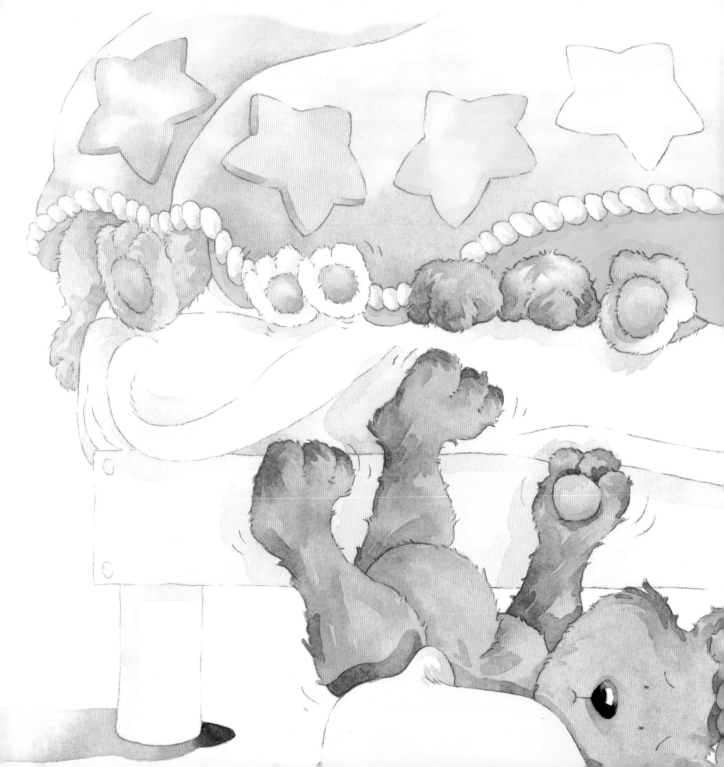

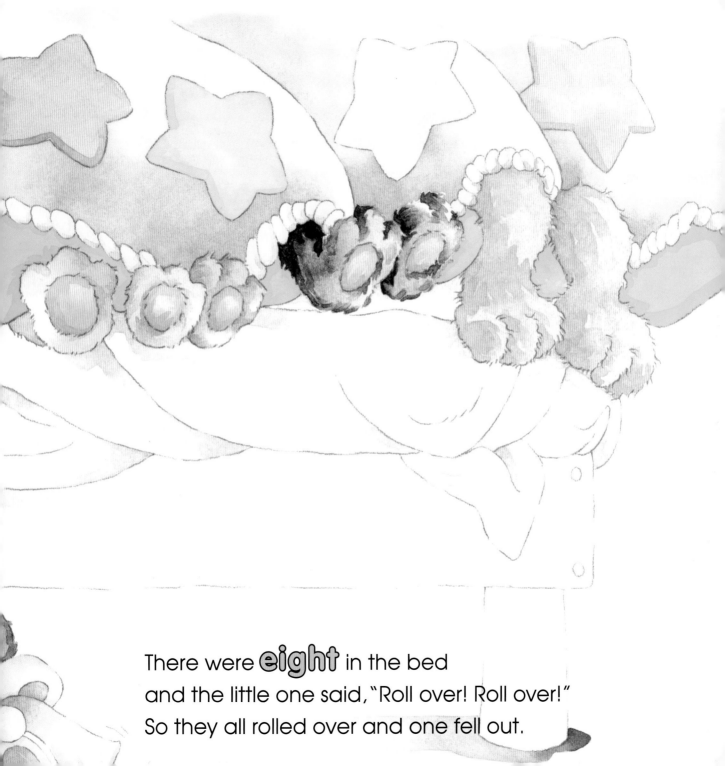

There were **eight** in the bed
and the little one said, "Roll over! Roll over!"
So they all rolled over and one fell out.

There were seven in the bed
and the little one said, "Roll over! Roll over!"
So they all rolled over and one fell out.

There were **six** in the bed
and the little one said, "Roll over! Roll over!"
So they all rolled over and one fell out.

There were five in the bed
and the little one said, "Roll over! Roll over!"
So they all rolled over and one fell out.

There were **four** in the bed
and the little one said, "Roll over! Roll over!"
So they all rolled over and one fell out.

There were three in the bed
and the little one said, "Roll over! Roll over!"
So they all rolled over and one fell out.

There were **two** in the bed
and the little one said, "Roll over! Roll over!"
So they all rolled over and one fell out.

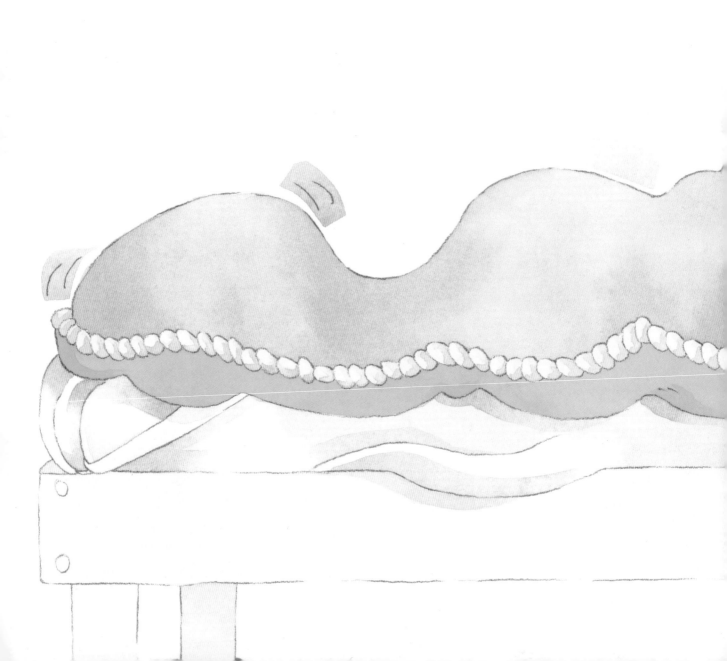

There was **one** in the bed
and the little one said, "Goodnight."

Count how many items are in each group. Practice counting together with a friend.

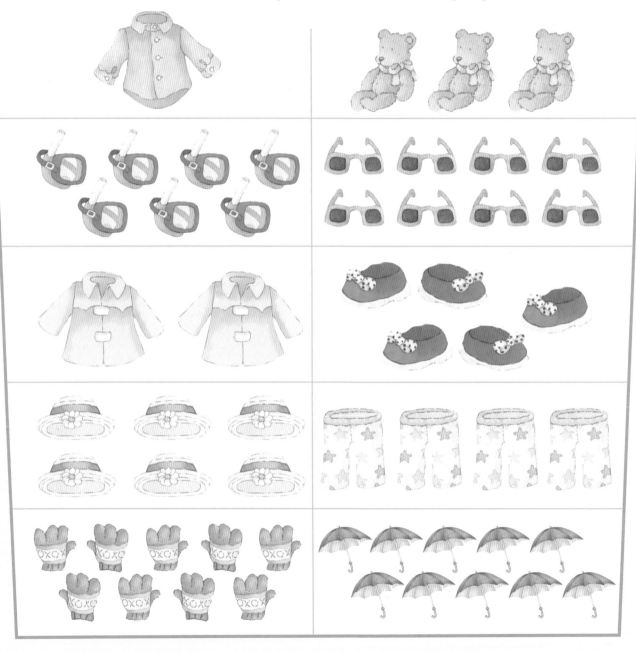